A Search for
TWO BAD MICE

BOOKS BY ELEANOR CLYMER

The Spider, the Cave and the Pottery Bowl
Santiago's Silver Mine
Chipmunk in the Forest
Harry the Wild West Horse
Horatio
Horatio's Birthday
Leave Horatio Alone
Horatio Goes to the Country
Horatio Solves a Mystery

A Search for
TWO BAD MICE

by ELEANOR CLYMER

Pictures by Margery Gill

ATHENEUM   1980   NEW YORK

LIBRARY OF CONGRESS CATALOGING IN PUBLICATION DATA

Clymer, Eleanor Lowenton, date
A search for two bad mice.

SUMMARY: When her younger sister threatens to ruin
the family's trip to England because of their cat,
Barbara finds a way to make the vacation a success.
[1. Vacations—Fiction. 2. Family life—Fiction.
3. England—Fiction] I. Gill, Margery.
II. Title.
PZ7.C6272Sg   [Fic]   80-21789
ISBN 0-689-30771-3

Published simultaneously in Canada by
McClelland & Stewart, Ltd.
Manufactured by The American Book/Stratford Press, Inc.
Saddle Brook, New Jersey
First Edition

Last summer my father had to go to England. There were some meetings he had to attend. We were disappointed. We had been planning to take a camping trip, all of us: me, Barbara; my sister Sarah; Mother and Father. Also our cat, Leo.

My mother said, "This is one summer we are going to spend together. Sarah is old enough to go, and Barbara is not too old."

Father said, "Well then, come along.

4

Let's all go to England."

I didn't want to go. I had never heard anything about it that made me want to go there.

Mother said, "You know all our history started there."

I said, "Like what?"

She said, "Well, you know about the Pilgrims."

Of course I knew about the Pilgrims. They had come to America from England because they wanted to get away from there.

Mother said, "George Washington's family came from there."

I said, "Yes, but he was the leader of the Revolution because we wanted our independence, and King George was very mean and said the Americans were a lot of rabble."

So Mother thought some more and said, "Well, lots of our greatest writers were English. Don't you want to see the places where they lived?"

"Like who?" I asked.

"Shakespeare, Milton, Dickens, Thackeray."

It sounded too much like homework.

Poor Mother. She went over to the bookcase and thought a while and then said, "Robin Hood!"

"Oh!" I said. I liked Robin Hood. Also Maid Marian.

Then Mother said, "King Arthur!"

Then we all started to get ideas. Guinevere. Lancelot. Dick Whittington. *Treasure Island. Wind in the Willows. Ivanhoe.* Jack the Giant Killer. London Bridge. Gulliver. Mary Poppins.

We thought of more and more names and they were all English.

Sarah was listening, and suddenly she said, "Hunca Munca and Tom Thumb."

They are the characters in her favorite book, *The Tale of Two Bad Mice.*

We were proud of her. When she saw

we were pleased, she said, "Peter Rabbit, Tom Kitten."

Mother said, "That's right, darling. And maybe, if Father gets through with his meetings in time, we'll go and see some of the places."

So we were very happy, until the question of Leo came up. Leo is big and yellow and has a big round face with fur all around it. He looks like a lion, that's why his name is Leo. We've had him since I was little. Now he is getting old, and Sarah takes care of him.

She asked, "Are we taking Leo?"

Mother said, "No, we can't. Mrs. Preston will look after him. She's right next door."

Sarah said she couldn't leave him. He would only eat if she fed him. We would have to take him along.

Father said, "We can't. They have a law over there. No animals can enter Britain. None whatever."

So Sarah said she wouldn't go either.

Father said, "We can't regulate our lives by a cat, even if he is old."

Sarah asked, "You wouldn't go and leave me if I was old, would you?"

Father said, "That's different. Anyhow you're not old, and won't be until I'm dead and gone."

Sarah began to cry. I thought, "This is going to be a fine trip, with that kid crying for Leo all the time."

To take her mind off Leo, I read to her. I read *Peter Rabbit* and *Tom Kitten,* and *The Tale of Two Bad Mice* three times.

The two bad mice are, as I said, Hunca Munca and Tom Thumb, who sneaked into a dollhouse and stole things. I always liked that story myself. I used to wish I had a dollhouse like the one in the pictures, and Sarah does, too. We told her that if we went to England we could see the one that belonged to Beatrix Potter, the lady who wrote the book.

She felt better and explained to Leo that Mrs. Preston would take good care of him, and she would bring him something nice.

Father grumbled, "Once that cat passes on, we are not getting any more animals. I want to be able to shut the door and go places."

But he didn't say it where Sarah could hear him.

So we got ready (school was over by this time) and went.

It was very exciting. I had been in a plane before but not across the ocean. When I looked down and saw the edge of the land way down there, and then the blue water with tiny boats on it, I was thrilled. Then we were flying above the clouds. They looked like a bed of fleecy feathers under the plane.

But you can't look out of the window

for six hours. So we ate and played games, and I read about Hunca Munca and Tom Thumb seven or eight times, and we had tea with biscuits (which are really cookies) and at last we saw land down below.

That was a thrill, too. Because in spite of my remarks about how the Pilgrims just wanted to get away from there, I couldn't help thinking: *This is the place they came from! They came in wooden boats across all those miles of water! How brave!*

We landed and got on a bus for London. After we found our seats, I looked out of the window and suddenly I screamed, "Father! They're driving on the wrong side of the road!"

Everybody in the bus laughed, and my face got red. Because of course they drive on the left in England. I got used to it after a while, but I never got used to crossing the street, because you have to look right instead of left to see if any cars are coming.

We went to our hotel, and Father regis-
tered. Then a man took our bags and said,
"The lift is this way."

He meant the elevator.

This kind of thing happened a great
many times until we learned about things.

We went up to our rooms and unpacked
and had a bath and clean clothes and went
down to the dining room for dinner.

There was a family at a table near ours. A father and mother and three children. The father ordered the dinner for all the children. He didn't ask them what they wanted, he just ordered. I watched to see if they would complain, but they didn't.

They ate in a funny way. Each one held his fork in the left hand and pushed the food onto the back of it with his knife. Then he ate off the fork, holding it upside down. I tried to do it, but the food all fell off.

Mother said, "Barbara! Wipe your fingers, please."

I said, "I need a clean napkin."

The waiter heard me and stared. Then he brought one and said, "Your serviette, Miss."

It turns out that a napkin in England is a baby's diaper. You don't ask for one in a restaurant.

For a week we stayed in London while

Father went to meetings. We went to Buck-
ingham Palace and saw them changing the
Guard. We went to the zoo and the Old
Curiosity Shop. We went to a museum and
saw Queen Mary's dollhouse.

That reminded Sarah. "When are we
going to see Hunca Munca and Tom
Thumb?"

Mother said, "Pretty soon. As soon as Father's meetings are finished."

But the meetings went on and on.

We went to the Tower of London and saw the Crown Jewels and the room where Mary Queen of Scots was kept prisoner.

We saw Madame Tussaud's waxworks.

We went to the British Museum and saw Magna Carta and the Rosetta Stone.

Sarah asked every day, "When are we going to see Hunca Munca and Tom Thumb?"

And every day Mother said, "Pretty soon."

Then one morning we went to American Express to get our mail, and there was a letter from home.

I said, "Oh, look, it's from Mrs. Preston."

I shouldn't have said it because Sarah exclaimed, "What does she say? How is Leo?"

So then we had to open it and read it to her. And it said: "Dear friends, I hope you are having a good time, I am doing the best I can with Leo, but he refuses to eat. I think he misses the little girl, for he just sleeps on her bed all the time. Well, don't worry, everything will be all right. Sincerely yours, Harriet Preston."

Then Sarah began to cry and said, "Let's go home. Leo will die if he doesn't eat."

Mother said, "Now stop that." But Sarah just cried harder.

I said, "The best thing is to go back to the hotel and read her about Hunca Munca

and Tom Thumb."

So we took a taxi back to the hotel. I forgot to say, the taxis in England are the greatest. They are black and high and you can walk into one standing up. When you arrive, the driver gets out and opens the door and says, "Thank you, Madam."

We went to our room and I got the book, but Sarah was too sad to listen. She had stopped crying, but she just sat with her chin in her hand and sniffed.

I said to Mother, "Let's go down and have tea." Because tea in an English hotel is special.

They bring you a pot of tea and the most luscious things to eat: bread and butter and biscuits (cookies) and teacake and cream and jam and honey. You would never be allowed to eat all that stuff at home so soon before dinner.

I ate like a pig, but Sarah hardly touched a thing. At last Father came and joined us. He was very pleased because his meetings were over and he had tickets to the theater.

The theater in London is the greatest because the play starts early, seven o'clock or half-past, so your parents have no excuse not to take you. Father had bought tickets to a play called *The Mousetrap,* which I had been dying to see. It's been running for more than twenty-five years. He said we would celebrate.

Then he looked at Sarah and asked,
"What's the matter?" So we told him about
Leo.

Father was furious. He said, "I told you
we could not regulate our lives by a cat."

Sarah said, "I want to go home tomorrow."

Father said, "We will not go home tomorrow. I have been working all this time,

and now we are going to have some fun."

But obviously it was not going to be any fun dragging a red-nosed, sniffling child about.

I had an idea. I said, "Sarah, we can't go home without seeing Hunca Munca and Tom Thumb. Even Leo wouldn't want you to miss that."

She nodded and said, "All right. Let's go there."

She agreed to go to the theater too, though at first she didn't want to see a play called *The Mousetrap,* till we explained that it wasn't to catch real mice.

The play was great. It was a real thriller, and I couldn't wait to tell my friends about it. Sarah fell asleep. It must be awful to be so young.

The next day, Father rented a car, and we started out. We had a map so we knew where Hunca Munca's house was. It was in the Lake Country.

I wanted to see where King Arthur was supposed to have lived, and Sherwood Forest where Robin Hood had his adventures. But Mother said, "We had better do Beatrix Potter. Maybe it will take her mind off Leo. We'll have time for King Arthur later."

So we drove north from London. Father had a little trouble keeping on the left side of the road. The roundabouts were the worst. They don't have too many traffic lights, but every so often you come to a roundabout. A traffic circle, actually. Then he wanted to keep to the right, and we all screamed, "Keep left! Keep left!"

Mother held the map, and I looked over her shoulder. The map of England is different from ours. There are no open spaces. It's all covered with roads and names of places.

You drive along past fields and gardens and sometimes between hedges so high you can't see over the top. Then you come to a village. Some of the villages are so old you think you're back in the Middle Ages. In some, the houses are in the middle of lovely gardens with a million flowers blooming. In other places the houses are built of stone and they have no front yards; the door opens right on the street. And the street is stone and

about two feet wide. And the roadway winds around between these little stone houses and is hardly wide enough for two cars to pass. Then all of a sudden along comes a lorry. (That's a truck.)

A couple of times Father drove right up on the sidewalk.

The places have interesting names. We went through Banbury (where the cross is) and Chipping Norton and Chipping Camden and Stowe-on-the-Wold and a place called Broadway. Then we came to Stratford-upon-Avon, where Shakespeare lived. Mother made us stop and look around. We saw Ann Hathaway's cottage and bought postcards.

We stopped in a shop to get some things for a picnic lunch. It's very interesting to shop in England.

You go to a grocery store and ask for some bread and cheese and the man puts them on the counter. Then you ask for milk and he says, "That is at the dairy, Madam."

You ask for apples and he says, "That is at the greengrocer's, Madam."

So you pay him and he says, "Thank you!" But he doesn't put your things in a bag.

Mother said, "Oh, dear, I forgot my shopping bag." So the man offered to sell her a shopping bag.

Sure enough, when we were out in the street, I saw that almost every woman was carrying a shopping bag. And an umbrella. Because you never know when it will rain.

It began to rain right then, and Mother said, "Go and sit in the car." She went on to the other stores, and when she came back, she had some meat pies that she had bought at the butcher's.

It rained hard. Father could hardly see through the windshield. (They call it the windscreen. The hood is a bonnet, the trunk is the boot, and gas is petrol. And is it expensive!)

We drove on to look for a place to have our picnic and also to wait for the rain to stop. But it didn't stop, so we pulled off the road and ate in the car.

We were tired. Father had said that we could get to the Lake Country in one day because it was only two hundred fifty miles.

At home you can drive two hundred fifty miles in four hours, but not in England. You have to watch out for sheep, and roundabouts, and keep on the left side of the road, and stop every few miles to look at something old.

England has had people living in it for thousands of years, and they all left something behind. Our house at home is about one hundred fifty years old. We thought it was an old house, but in England that would be new.

We looked for a place to stay for the night. A sign in a window said BED AND BREAKFAST.

"Bed and Breakfast" is the greatest. I like it better than a hotel because it is somebody's house and you don't have to dress up for dinner. This place was small and cozy. There was a garden with a million flowers. The sun came out as we got to the door, and the whole place looked like a rainbow.

We went in, and the lady made a fire because it was damp. She gave us tea and let us watch her TV, or telly as she called it.

There was a cricket game on. The men stood around on the grass wearing white shirts and pants, and now and then they swatted a ball with a flat bat, and somebody said, "Jolly good!" I couldn't figure out what they were trying to do.

The next morning we went on to the Lake Country.

I soon saw why it was called that. Wherever you went there were lakes. And hills. It could have been called the Hill Country just as well. It was really beautiful.

We got out of the car and stood on a hill overlooking a lake. There were white clouds in the blue sky and the wind was blowing and making ripples on the lake.

2103751

Mother said, "In spring there would be daffodils!" And she began to quote poetry:

"I wandered lonely as a cloud
   That floats on high o'er dales and hills,
When all at once I saw a crowd,
   A host, of golden daffodils;
Beside the lake, beneath the trees,
Fluttering and dancing in the breeze.

Continuous as the stars that shine
   And twinkle on the Milky Way —"

"Mother," I said.

"That was Wordsworth," she said. "We could go to see the house where he lived."

Sarah said, "What about Hunca Munca and Tom Thumb?"

Father gave a sigh and looked at the map and said, "Come on, everybody."

So we drove some more, till we came to a village. Then we went on till we came to a

house and a sign outside that said Hill Top.
We had arrived.

We went in. The ceiling was low, and
in the middle of the room was a table with
little books on it, just like the little books I
had been reading to Sarah.

Sarah looked all around and smiled. It was the first time she had smiled in days.

She looked up at the lady who was in charge and asked, "Where is the dollhouse?"

"Upstairs," said the lady. And Sarah started up the stairs. The rest of us followed. We peeped into the bedrooms on the way. They were small and neat, just like the pictures in the books.

And then, in the front bedroom, we saw the dollhouse. Sarah sat down on the floor. She put out her hand. Then she pulled it back. I could see she was dying to reach in and play with the furniture and the dolls, but she didn't. She knew it was not allowed. I wanted to myself, it was so lovely. There were muslin curtains at the windows, and inside you could see the kitchen and the parlor and the bedrooms, with the dolls standing stiffly and staring out at us.

Father and Mother waited for us to finish looking. Then Father sighed, pulled the little book out of his pocket, and sat down on the floor beside us and began to read.

"Once upon a time there was a very beautiful doll's house: It was red brick with white windows, and it had real muslin curtains and a front door and a chimney."

He read on and on, and some more
people who had come to visit the house stood
in the doorway and listened. When he was
through, he closed the book, stood up, and
bowed to the people, and they clapped and
laughed.

"Come on now," said Mother. "We still have to find a place to stay."

Sarah didn't want to leave.

"I want to see Hunca Munca and Tom Thumb," she said.

"But they aren't real mice," I told her. "They are just in the story."

"Oh, no!" she told me. "They are real. They live here. But I guess they wouldn't come out with so many people here."

I was surprised. I didn't know she *believed* in them, the way she believed in Santa Claus and the Easter Bunny.

We went down the stairs and out into the garden. I didn't want to leave either. I thought how nice it would be to live here in this darling little house and have rabbits and guinea pigs and kittens to play with, and perhaps a pig and a couple of dogs.

We got in the car and drove some more till we saw a bed and breakfast sign. It was a farmhouse, bigger than Hill Top.

It was built of stone, and the roof came
down low over the front door. An old man
was sitting on a stone wall feeding two lambs
out of milk bottles.

Mother knocked at the door. The man
said, "You wants to pull the bell." So she
pulled at a knob, and we heard it echoing
somewhere deep inside.

A woman came, wiping her hands on her apron. She had red cheeks, and she pushed her hair back with her hand. She said there were two bedrooms vacant, and supper was in half an hour. So we went in.

The hall floor was stone. A door opened into a parlor where some people were sitting in front of a fire. We went up to the bed-rooms. The windows were wide open, and it was freezing.

Mother asked if there was any heat, and the woman said, yes, the electric heater was right there, and you put in a shilling, but she didn't think it was really cold. As soon as she went away, Father closed the windows and turned on the heater. We washed our faces and brushed our hair and went down to the parlor and sat by the fire.

An English family was there, a father and mother and two girls, one my age, and one about six. They said, "How d'you do" to us and introduced themselves, saying, "You're American, aren't you?"

I wondered how they knew, since we hadn't said a word so far. Then the mother, whose name was Mrs. Patton, said, "Alice said you had asked for a heater. Americans often find it cold here." Alice was the older girl. She had been upstairs when we went up.

The littler girl was Gillian, and she and Sarah became instant friends. I could see poor Sarah heave a sigh of relief at finding someone her own size at last.

They sat on the floor and talked. Alice and I talked, and our parents compared maps and bed and breakfast places.

When Mrs. Robertson, the landlady, came to announce that supper was ready, we all went in together. There were several other people, and we all sat around a big table and passed the plates around. There was roast beef and Yorkshire pudding and the most wonderful bread and butter, and trifle for a sweet (that means dessert). The trifle was cake with strawberries and thick cream. Once more I ate like a pig. Even Sarah was hungry.

After supper Alice and I helped carry the plates out, and I saw the kitchen. It was built of stone, and there was a spring in it. The water came out of a pipe into a stone basin and ran off like a brook down the mid-

dle of the floor. It was freezing cold in there too, but the women who were working there had their sleeves rolled up and didn't even have goose pimples.

47

I asked how old the house was. Mrs. Robertson said, "The barn is from the twelfth century, but this house was built in the thirteenth."

I said, "And I thought *we* lived in an old house!"

We went out to see the barn. It was stone too, and inside were the two lambs the farmer had been feeding, and our two sisters sitting in some hay and playing with—you guessed it—two kittens. One was yellow and one was gray with stripes.

"The gray one is Tom Kitten," Sarah told me.

"How do you know?" I asked.

"Can't you see?" she asked.

Alice and I walked out. "I'm so glad you came," she said. "I was going out of my mind with Gillian."

"The same here with Sarah," I said, and we grinned at each other. Alice was a really nice girl. We went for a walk up a hill. It was after eight o'clock, but it was still very light. It didn't really get dark till after ten.

On the top of the hill was a ring of standing stones.

"What's that for?" I asked.

"The early Britons put them there,"

Alice said. "I suppose they worshipped there. There are lots of those stone circles."

"Like Stonehenge," I said. "We went to see it."

I shivered. I wasn't cold, but it was scary to think how old England was.

"The country people used to think witches met here," Alice said. "Come on, let's go back to the house."

We went back and played Scrabble. Sarah and Gillian had brought the kittens in and were playing house. Our parents were talking, happy to have some adults for company.

The next day we had to go back to Hill Top. Sarah had told Gillian about the dollhouse and she had to see it. Gillian's mother bought her a copy of *The Tale of Two Bad Mice*.

Again Sarah didn't want to leave. "You can all go," she said. "Me and Gillian will stay here. If we sit quiet, the mice will come out."

Fortunately the lady in charge said they were closing, so we had to leave.

This went on for several days. I was wondering when we would go to look for King Arthur's castle. But Sarah and Gillian were so happy that we stayed on at the farm.

"Anything for a quiet life," Father said. And Mr. Patton agreed with him.

One day we took a picnic lunch and all went off into the mountains. The Pattons took care of the lunch. When English people take a picnic, they are serious about it. They had a stove, a teakettle, a teapot, a bottle of milk, a basket with sandwiches and cold chicken, and for dessert, strawberries. And cheese. Some English people think cheese is as good as a sweet. I don't.

Alice and I talked about school and

hockey and sailing and the books we liked. Can you imagine, her favorites were the Little House books! And she liked stories about what she called Red Indians. She was surprised when I said they'd rather be called Native Americans.

On the way home we stopped at Hill Top to see the dollhouse again. Our parents didn't go in. They had seen enough of it. Sarah and Gillian were dying to play with it. But Alice and I told them sternly what would happen if they dared to touch. So they peered into every window, and finally had to be dragged away.

"If we could only see Hunca Munca and Tom Thumb just once!" Sarah said sadly. I did feel sorry for her. It's hard to be little.

In the evening they played with their kittens again.

At last we were going to have to leave. It was time to go home. The next morning we were to drive back to London and fly home from Heathrow Airport. But first we would pay one more visit to Hill Top. We planned to drive there, and the Pattons would follow in their car. Then after one last look, we would say goodbye. I was so fond of Alice by now that I could hardly bear the idea.

Sarah didn't want to leave Gillian, and even more important, she still hadn't given up hope of seeing the mice.

"We'll have trouble getting her away," I said to Alice. "She's just crazy about those mice. Why, in London she didn't want to go to see *The Mousetrap*."

Then Alice and I got our great idea, both at once. It was what they call two minds with but a single thought.

"Mousetrap!" we both exclaimed.

"Where can we get one?" I asked.

"I know. Follow me," said Alice.

She led the way to the kitchen.

It was the middle of the afternoon, so

nobody was in the kitchen. Sure enough, on a shelf was a big mousetrap, the kind that catches them alive and doesn't hurt them.

Alice took it and put it under her jacket.

It was very wicked of us, and we knew we shouldn't be doing it. Besides, we weren't at all sure it would work unless we were very lucky.

"Have you got any food in your room?" Alice asked. "I don't like to sneak their food."

I knew we had biscuits and cheese so I got some. We went to the barn, set up the mousetrap in a dark corner, baited it with goodies, and went away.

All that evening we were so jittery we could hardly sit still.

"Let's go for a walk," I said.

Our parents didn't mind. The sun had gone down, but the sky was still light and the moon was shining.

"But remember we have to be ready to leave tomorrow. So get back in time to pack," Mother said.

We walked up the hill to the stone circle. The moonlight was so bright that the stones cast a shadow on the ground.

"It's spooky," I said. "I keep expecting witches to come out from behind the stones."

"And here we are!" said a scary voice. A hunched figure shuffled toward us.

I screamed, "Eek!" and started to run.

Then about six more of them came out,
laughing like anything. They were just a
bunch of teen-agers playing around on the
hill.

"Watch out or we'll put a spell on you!"
one of them said.

"You startled us," said Alice with dignity. "Come on, we must be going."

We walked down the hill, listening to those teen-agers laughing at us and feeling foolish.

"Shall we look at the trap?" I suggested, to change the subject.

We went cautiously into the barn, hoping nobody would see us.

"The coast is clear," said Alice. "The farmer's gone to bed."

We crept in and looked at the mouse-trap. There was one little mouse in it, brown with big ears.

"Better leave it there," Alice said. "Maybe another one will join it."

We went back to the house and packed and went to bed.

The next morning we got up at dawn. I had a small cardboard box with holes punched in the top. We tiptoed to the door.

Mrs. Robertson saw us. "Where are you

girls going so early?" she asked.

"We just want to say goodbye to the lambs and the kittens," I said. "We wish we didn't have to go."

"We'll be sorry to see you go," she said. "Here, have a bun to hold you till breakfast."

Munching our buns, we went to the barn and hurried to the corner.

"What luck!" said Alice. "Two of them!"

While I held the box, she opened the trap and dumped the mice in. I had put some bits of bread and cheese in the box. I hoped they wouldn't be too scared to eat them.

"It's only for a little while," I told them,
"and it's for a good cause."

I put the box in my flight bag.

After breakfast, we said goodbye to the
Robertsons and started out. Sarah and Gillian
were together in the Pattons' car, and Alice
and I were in ours.

When we got to Hill Top, Father said,
"Now you girls all go up and say one last
farewell, and don't be too long about it."

62

We climbed out, and the little girls joined us. I noted that Sarah was carrying her flight bag.

"What's that for?" I asked.

She shrugged. "I just like to carry it," she said. "You've got yours."

There was nothing I could say to that.

The lady at the desk smiled at us. "You know the way," she said.

I went ahead. Alice dawdled on the stairs, telling Gillian and Sarah that they should look at everything because they wouldn't be seeing it again. She made them go in the different rooms and look at the pictures on the walls.

When they came to the room with the dollhouse I was ready. I stood at the door and whispered, "Come and look. But be very very quiet. There's a surprise." I pointed.

The two little girls tiptoed in. They peered into the dollhouse. Then Sarah gasped and clapped her hands over her mouth in order not to scream.

"They're real!" she whispered. "I knew it!"

The two mice were scurrying around inside the dollhouse making scratchy noises. They were looking for the exit.

Then something else happened. Sarah leaned forward to get a better look. Her flight bag fell open. A furry head appeared. It was the gray kitten. It heard the scratching noise, and before we could stop it, it leaped out of the bag and straight into the dollhouse.

"Squeak!" The mice disappeared. The dollhouse rocked. The kitten tried to get out, but it had forgotten the way. Everything was

knocked over. The dolls lay on their backs
and smiled.

"Sarah!" I scolded. "You bad girl!
What's the idea?"

But I didn't say it too loud because I
didn't want anybody to come. Alice and Gillian and Sarah were almost bursting, trying
not to laugh. They were hysterical.

Somebody had to take charge. With great presence of mind, I reached in and grabbed the kitten. I stuffed her into the flight bag and gave it to Alice. Then I closed the door, so that nobody should hear us.

"Now," I said, "you two, put everything to rights. And fast!"

Of course, they were glad to do it. Carefully they picked up the furniture and stood it upright. They put the lamps and the dishes where they belonged. They put the dolls to bed. After all, they had had a great shock and needed to rest.

At last they were finished.

"Come along," I said.

Very quietly we went down the stairs. We said goodbye to the lady at the desk, keeping our faces as straight as we could.

"Thank you for everything," I said. "We're going home now."

"It's been lovely to have you," she said. "Have a safe journey. Goodbye."

Then as we reached the door, I couldn't help saying, "Oh, by the way, we saw a couple of mice up there."

"Really!" said the lady. "People must have been dropping crumbs. I must set—"

I knew she was going to say she would set a trap, and then Sarah would howl.

I interrupted. "Yes, we think they were Hunca Munca and Tom Thumb. Goodbye!" And we rushed out the door.

We said goodbye to the Pattons. We promised to write, and we invited them to come to see us in America. And they said the next time we must visit them at their house and we would surely see King Arthur's Castle and Sherwood Forest.

I thought Sarah and Gillian would be crying at the thought of separating, but they weren't. Their faces were filled with joy.

"We saw them, didn't we?" Sarah said to Gillian.

Alice and I grinned at each other.

We got into our car. Father started the
motor. Suddenly Sarah gave a shriek.

"My flight bag!" Alice was still holding
it.

"Oh!" she said, and she tossed the bag
through the open window into Sarah's arms.
At last we were off.

I wondered what I ought to do. It was my duty to tell Father what I knew. But then there would be wails and tears all the way back to London. I kept quiet. After all, I was not entirely blameless myself.

It wasn't until we stopped for lunch that Sarah, so to speak, let the cat out of the bag.

She had to, because by that time it was yelling and scratching.

Father exploded. "How dare you take that kitten away from the farm!" he demanded. "And now it's too late to take it back."

"It's for Leo," said Sarah. "I promised to bring him a present. Can I please give him some milk?"

The waitress brought a saucer of milk and a piece of string so Sarah could take the kitten for a walk.

While she was walking, Mother said, "You know, it may not be a bad idea. In case Leo has passed away."

Father growled. "But I said *no more animals.*"

However, he seemed to be outnumbered.

I asked, "Is it allowed to take animals out of England?"

He said, "Yes. Wish it weren't."

In London there was a letter from Mrs. Preston. She said Leo was very thin, but was still hanging on. She hoped he would revive when we returned.

We bought a carrier for the kitten. He was very good and slept most of the way across the Atlantic.

I asked Sarah how she had had the nerve to do such a naughty thing as to go off with a kitten.

She said, "I thought if we didn't see Hunca Munca and Tom Thumb at least I could have Tom Kitten. But I didn't mean to scare them. I hope they got over it. And now I know they live there."

I thought maybe it was wrong of me to have fooled her. Then I decided. Well, after all, she does believe in Santa Claus and the Easter Bunny. Why not the two bad mice?

We still had one more crisis to face. What if Leo wasn't there when we arrived? But

when we walked in, there he was, purring
and rubbing against Sarah's legs as though
she had just come home from school.

"Look, Leo," she said. "See what I
brought you!" and she let Tom Kitten out of
the carrier.

Father had said Leo was too old to adjust to having a young kitten in the house, but he liked Tom Kitten very much. He licked him all over, and they both curled up in Father's chair.

That was a year ago, and Leo is as healthy as can be. But the kitten turned out to be a girl, so we called her Tomasina. She grew up and had a family, and now we have five.

And for Christmas, Father is building us a dollhouse. He says, though, "NO MICE."

There's just one more thing. This story should really be called, *The Tale of Four Bad Girls.*